T0198796

It's All About Being Brave

Written by Rebecca Klar Lusk

Illustrated by Robert E. Klar

WestBow Press books may be ordered through booksellers or by contacting:

WestBow Press
A Division of Thomas Nelson & Zondervan
1663 Liberty Drive
Bloomington, IN 47403
www.westbowpress.com
1 (866) 928-1240

ISBN: 978-1-9736-7881-6 (sc)
ISBN: 978-1-9736-7882-3 (e)

Library of Congress Control Number: 2019917587

Print information available on the last page.

WestBow Press rev. date: 11/1/2019

WestBow
PRESS®
A DIVISION OF THOMAS NELSON
& ZONDERVAN

This book belongs to

_____

From

_____

For Eli Truman Lusk and Everly Christine Lusk, my treasured grandchildren.

This, the sixth "It's All About" book, is another reminder that whether you're Tall, Small, Strong, Tough, Smart, or Brave, It's All About Jesus in your heart!

Each book honors the life and memory of my son, Christopher Paul Lusk, as he truly demonstrated the love of Jesus in his heart. He loved serving the Lord, and fully believed that God created and loved each of us as unique individuals. Chris demonstrated powerful bravery as he journeyed through illness that led him to his heavenly home at a young age. He truly was a remarkable young man.

You are loved unconditionally by your creator. May you know Him personally in your heart.

Honoring the Brave

With this book, I want to give two special people honor for their service and bravery: my uncle, Robert "Bob" Klar, and my aunt, Beth Ann Moore Klar. Both of them served God and country during WWII and were an inspiration to many throughout their lives. Bob enlisted in the U.S. Army and was part of the 148th Combat Engineers. He was one of many brave men who helped build the bridges in Europe needed to aid the Allies in transportation. His role in helping to build a pontoon bridge over the Rhine at Remagen, Germany, was one of his proudest accomplishments.

Beth Ann Moore enlisted in the Army Nurse Corps as a 2nd Lieutenant and served in the U.S. before being assigned to duty overseas in the Pacific. While there, she was promoted to 1st Lieutenant.

These two brave veterans met and were married after the war and were committed to God and each other. They celebrated over 60 years together, and their faith in God, and their journey on this earth impacted many lives in powerful ways.

My brother, Robert Klar is Uncle Bob's namesake. He and I are so blessed to have had these two individuals in our lives.

Rebecca Klar Lusk

"It's all about being brave," said the lion cub,
To everyone he met.
"It's all about being brave that's important,
And don't you ever forget."

"Being brave I can face others
Who have their fear of me.
Since I'm known as a <u>fearless</u> king,
They'd rather turn away and flee."

2

"Because I'm brave, I watch them shake.
My size doesn't even matter.
I loudly roar with all my might,
And quickly they all scatter."

3

"I'm not afraid of my enemies.
I'll challenge them with a dare.
They know I won't back down.
In their eyes I bravely stare."

4

"It doesn't matter what the day brings,
With each adventure I'll be bold.
I have no cause to be frightened.
Lions have <u>courage</u>, I've been told."

"When others are scared, I watch in awe.
They're timid, concerned, and weak.
They seem afraid of all those around,
And it's shelter that they seek."

6

"Of all the lions in my <u>pride</u>,
I'm more daring than all the rest.
I venture out to face any danger,
Be it north, south, east, or west."

7

"Being **brave** makes me
feel better than others.
I smirk and don't back down.
They dash off with their friends,
Instead of hanging around"

"It's all about being brave," said the cub,
As a large dark shadow appeared.
He was startled and looked to see
An angry elephant was coming near.

"I'm not afraid," said the lion,
As the elephant stomped on the ground.
The rumble was so loud, the ground shook,
And the lion couldn't make a sound.

The elephant <u>trumpeted</u>, "You're not so **brave**!

You're so scared you better retreat.

I say it's all about being **BIG**.

I could trample you with one of my feet!"

11

God tells us in His Word that all of us are special. Being brave is not the best thing, for God loves each and every one of us just the way we are. After all, God made us. We are His creation, and He is the maker of all good things. Be yourself, and be thankful for all that you are. God loves each of us unconditionally. That means His love for us will never change.

He sent His son to die for us on a cross. It's really ALL ABOUT KNOWING JESUS. He gives us what we need. Jesus and God His father are a team. If you haven't asked Jesus into your heart, do it right now. Accepting Jesus as your personal Lord and Savior is the most important life decision you will ever make. Through Him you have eternal life. That's a life that goes on forever in heaven.

Hallelujah for
JESUS!

Vocabulary

1. Important – Meaningful and valuable.
2. Fearless – Not afraid, very brave.
3. Scatter – Separate, go in different directions.
4. Challenge – To compete and prove your ability.
5. Courage – The ability to do something difficult.
6. Timid – Shy, lack of self-confidence.
7. Pride – A group of lions.
8. Smirk – Smile in an unpleasant or silly way.
9. Startled – Surprised, frightened suddenly.
10. Rumble – Make a low, heavy, continuous sound.
11. Trumpeted – Made a sound like a trumpet.

Praise and Prayer

Give God Praise if you are BRAVE.
That's how He created you.
He designed you with much love
And He knows what you can do.

Always remember, He looks inside
To see what's in your heart.
He desires for you to accept Jesus,
And never grow apart.

It's really all about knowing JESUS
That matters most of all.
God wants you to accept His Son,
Whether you're tough, strong, smart, small, or tall.

Invite Jesus into your heart today.
Say this simple prayer.
Just be how God created you.
And serve Him everywhere.

Dear Jesus,

I need you in my life. I know you died for me on the cross because of your love for me. Come into my life and live in my heart. Forgive me for the things I have done wrong. I want to follow you and know more about you. You have done something wonderful for me. Let me live for you. Thank you, Amen.

All About Me

My full name is_____.

I was born in_____.

I will be_____ years old.

My favorite color is _____.

I like to learn about_____.

My best friend(s) is(are)_____.

My favorite wild animal is the _____.

If I could travel anywhere, I would go to _____.

I felt very BRAVE when I_____.

I like to help others by_____.

When I grow up I would like to be_____.

Three things I enjoy doing are_____.

_____,

and_____.

Be Brave----Do It

Things to do and talk about with your family and friends

Visit a Veterans Museum, or research one together.

Meet and talk with veterans in your area.

Write a letter or help someone who is now serving in the military. See Operation Gratitude for contacts, ways, and means. www.operationgratitude.com

Find movies and books about being brave. Watch and read them together. Talk about how they make you feel.

Discuss fears that you would like to overcome.

Work on this together, make a plan, and be BRAVE.

Think of ways you can help others in your community, church, school, etc. Examples: Donate clothes, shoes, toys to places who shelter the homeless; pick up litter; find a military family in your neighborhood, and think of ways to bless them.

Design a T-shirt with a message that includes the word BRAVE

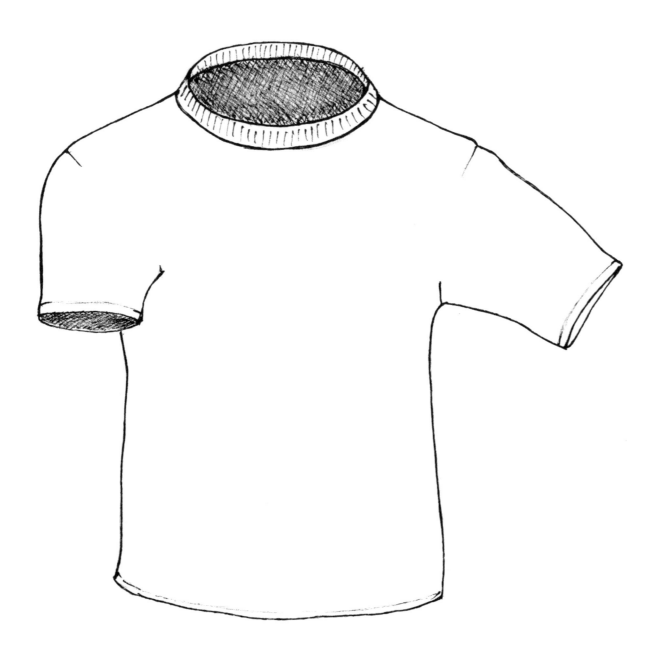

I'm Wild About These Animals

Think of some of your favorite jungle animals. Can you identify these ten by filling in the blanks below?

1. _a_t_og
2. _i_er
3. _l_p_a_t
4. _o_k_y
5. _i_n
6. _eb_a
7. _ir_f_e
8. _ye_a
9. _e_p_rd
10. _ip_o

Printed in the United States
By Bookmasters